THE BOLDS'

Christmas
Cracker

Look out for other books
by Julian Clary & David Roberts:

The Bolds

The Bolds to the Rescue

The Bolds on Holiday

The Bolds in Trouble

The Bolds Go Wild

The Bolds' Great Adventure
(A World Book Day Book)

Andersen Press • London

THE BOLDS'

Christmas Cracker

By Julian Clary

**Illustrated by
David Roberts**

First published in the UK in 2019 by
Andersen Press Limited
20 Vauxhall Bridge Road
London SW1V 2SA
www.andersenpress.co.uk

2 4 6 8 10 9 7 5 3 1

British Library Cataloguing in Publication Data available.

ISBN 978 1 78344 842 5

Printed and bound in China

THE BOLDS'

Christmas
Cracker

This book belongs to:

. . . .

. . . .

Well ho-ho-hello there, and welcome to

The Bolds' Christmas Cracker!

As you probably know, the Bolds are a very jolly family indeed, and so of course, they absolutely adore Christmas. Eating lots of delicious food, spending time with friends and family and, best of all, plenty of hyena laughter.

And now they've made this book for you, so you can have lots of Bolds festive fun of your own, even if you haven't had an invitation to 41 Fairfield Road itself. My my, aren't *you* a lucky pup?

Now, there is lots to do in here, so don't get overwhelmed! You have a whole twelve days of Christmas, and plenty more time besides. There are things to draw, puzzles to solve, codes to crack and stories to write! And you might find that Mr Bold has sprinkled one or two (or one hundred and two) of his own special cracker jokes throughout.

So all in all this should keep you very busy indeed, and help you to avoid dull comments from grown-ups about watching too much television and only boring people getting bored. I do hope you enjoy it.

Merry Christmas and happy puzzling!

Julian Clary

MEET THE BOLDS

I do hope you know by now who the Bolds are. If not, then you've been missing out on lots of fun! But in case you've forgotten in all the excitement of Christmassy hubbub, I'll make some quick introductions.

The Bolds are a family of hyenas, but you mustn't tell anyone that! They now live a (mostly) human life in Teddington, and try to keep animal antics to a minimum.

★ Mrs Bold has a market stall of unusual hats made from things like egg boxes and chicken bones.

★ Mr Bold writes the jokes that go inside Christmas crackers.

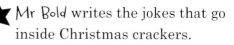

Bobby and **Betty Bold** are twin pups, and like running around and causing mayhem at home and school.

Uncle Tony is an elderly hyena, and likes to play dominoes and look after **Miranda** the cheeky monkey.

Mr McNumpty lives next door. He's really a grizzly bear with a glamorous past, but now he lives a quieter life.

MEET THE AUTHOR

Name: Julian Clary.

Birthday: 25th May.

Grew up in: Teddington.

Occupation: Author, actor and comedian.

Animals: Loves animals and has lots, including dogs, cats, ducks and chickens.

Clothes: Loves to dress up in extravagant costumes.

Loves: Touring the country, reading his books aloud to children and making people laugh.

Fun fact: Has been a contestant on *Strictly Come Dancing* and won *Celebrity Big Brother*.

MEET THE ILLUSTRATOR

Name: David Roberts.

Birthday: 8th May.

Grew up in: Liverpool.

Occupation: Artist and
writer.

Animals: Loves cats, but is scared of dogs.

Clothes: Likes to knit his own socks.

Loves: Drawing animals and clothes and hats, and
animals in clothes and hats!

Fun fact: Used to live in Hong Kong and work as
a milliner, which means he made hats, like Mrs
Bold!

MEET ME

Write a fact file about yourself

Name: ....

Birthday: ....

Lives in: ....

....

Family: ....

....

Animals: ....

....

Clothes: ....

....

Favourite hobbies: ....

....

Fun facts: ....

....

....

Draw a picture of yourself here.

SPOT THE
DIFFERENCE

Bobby and Betty have been messing around with some holiday snaps! Can you find 10 things they've changed?

Answers on page 168

TRUE OR FALSE

The Bolds have so many friends that things can get confusing! Can you figure out if these statements about them are true or false?

True / False

True	False	
✓	☐	1) The Bolds were invited to Buckingham Palace.
☐	✗	2) Fred's father is called Imamu.
☐	✗	3) Fifi Lampadaire is a famous actress.
✓	☐	4) On holiday, Bobby disguised himself as a dog.
☐	✗	5) Minnie is secretly a meerkat.
✓	☐	6) Mr McNumpty lived with an Arabian prince.
✓	☐	7) A turtle lived in the Bolds' washing machine.
☐	✗	8) Jeffrey Dobson wants to be a hyena.
☐	✗	9) Mr McNumpty and Minnie are very talented surfers.
☐	✗	10) The Bolds are friends with a goose called Happy.

answers on page 168

10

WORDSEARCH

Uncle Tony love s learning about human Christmas, but he still sometimes gets his letters muddled up! Can you help him find all the festive words?

S	T	R	D	F	Z	K	B	I	P	I	R	I	Y	P
N	L	B	M	M	M	I	V	R	A	J	B	K	U	T
R	D	L	M	I	N	C	E	P	I	E	S	A	L	I
Y	E	P	E	Y	S	S	K	O	A	O	C	J	E	N
A	G	K	E	B	E	T	G	N	I	K	C	O	T	S
D	B	M	C	N	E	N	L	F	R	I	I	S	I	E
I	L	A	T	A	I	L	A	E	E	U	E	U	D	L
L	P	S	U	D	R	M	G	K	T	N	H	A	E	T
O	R	V	D	B	I	C	A	N	T	O	H	L	Q	R
H	L	U	R	L	L	L	E	A	I	N	E	C	J	Q
M	P	G	Y	I	F	E	Y	O	J	J	Q	A	I	I
E	H	K	F	W	E	K	U	O	J	K	E	T	Q	P
N	I	O	O	S	P	A	B	W	J	L	U	N	F	I
P	Z	N	Y	L	L	O	H	U	J	O	I	A	L	M
Z	S	C	A	R	O	L	S	S	I	Y	P	S	I	S

YULETIDE	CAROLS	SANTA CLAUS	STOCKING
CRACKER	JOY	HOLLY	PUDDING
SNOWFLAKE	MINCE PIES	BAUBLE	FAMILY
PRESENTS	HOLIDAY	TINSEL	JINGLE BELLS
			MISTLETOE

12

answers on page 169

WORD SUDOKU

Bobby got a sudoku book in his stocking, and is now trying to make his own puzzle with words.

	O		D
		B	
	L		
O		D	

Can you fill in the grid so that every row, column and 2x2 square contains each letter from BOLD?

answers on page 169

MR BOLD'S JOKES

Mr Bold loves his job at the Christmas cracker factory!
Here are some Christmas jokes that he thinks are his best work.

Who looks after Father
Christmas when he's ill?
The National Elf Service.

What do you call a man who
claps at Christmas?
Santapplause.

Did Rudolph go to school?
No, he was elf-taught.

If a reindeer lost his tail, where
would he go for a new one?
A re-tail shop.

Why do the reindeer love
Father Christmas so much?
Because he fawns over them.

What did Father Christmas
say when Mrs Claus asked
about the weather?
'Looks like rain, dear.'

What is Rudolph's favourite day
of the year?
Red Nose Day.

What goes 'Oh! Oh! Oh!'?
Father Christmas walking
backwards.

How would you describe a
rich elf?
Welfy.

Who is the most famous elf?
Elfvis.

How many elves does it take to change a light bulb?
Ten. One to change it and nine to stand on each other's shoulders to reach it.

If there were eleven elves, and another one came along, what would he be?
The twelf.

What do wizards use to wrap their presents?
Spellotape.

Who delivers presents to sharks at Christmas?
Santa Jaws.

What did the dog get for Christmas?
A mobile bone.

Who is a child's favourite King?
Stoc-King.

'Can I have a broken drum for Christmas?'
'The best thing you could have asked for. You can't beat it.'

CAN YOU DRAW
A HYENA?

This is how David
Roberts draws
them...

Now it's
your turn!

MUDDLED MEALS

Mealtimes at Lotsfield Road can sometimes get a bit messy.
Can you unscramble these letters to help write
the Pets' Christmas dinner menu?

RYKETU

....

GINFFSUT

....

IKSERRHOY UGDINDP

....

....

18

answers on
page 170

SGPI NI EBLANSTK

....

....

PORSTUS

....

OPOTASET

....

ELYU OLG

....

GLOBAL GREETINGS

Mr McNumpty wants to wish all his friends
around the world a 'Merry Christmas'.

(A)	Feliz Navidad	(1)	Afrikaans
(B)	Mele Kalikimaka	(2)	Welsh
(C)	Joyeux Noël	(3)	Spanish
(D)	Merii Kurisumasu	(4)	Turkish
(E)	Geseënde Kersfees	(5)	Arabic
(F)	Mutlu Noeller	(6)	Japanese
(G)	Nadolig Llaween	(7)	French
(H)	Wesołych Świąt	(8)	Hawaiian
(I)	Eid Milad Saeid	(9)	Korean
(J)	Sung Tan Chuk Ha	(10)	Polish

COMIC CAPERS

Emergency drill! The Bolds have lots of animal friends visiting Fairfield Road when suddenly there's a human knock at the door.

Draw in the boxes what happens next.

KNOCK
KNOCK

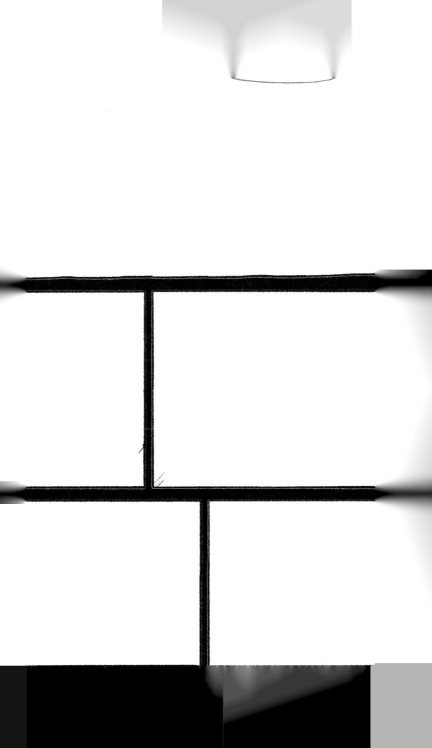

WHAT'S IN THE TOILET?

A very confused Mrs Bold can hear some splashing
sounds coming from *inside* the toilet.

Draw what you think could be in there.

CRYPTIC CODES

The Bolds are on an undercover mission,
and can only communicate in code. Can you
crack this one to discover a fun fact?

A	B	C	D	E	F	G	H	I
22	5	24	17	8	16	21	2	13

J	K	L	M	N	O	P	Q	R
23	19	9	15	6	7	25	12	18

S	T	U	V	W	X	Y	Z	
1	11	26	20	14	4	3	10	

__ __ __ __ __ __ __ __ __   __ __ __   __ __
24 2 18 13 1 11 15 22 1   14 22 1   15 18

__ __ __ __ ' __   __ __ __ __ __ __ __ __ __ __
5 7 9 17 ' 1   16 22 20 7 26 18 13 11 8

__ __ __ __   __ __   __ __ __ __
11 13 15 8   7 16   3 8 22 18

answer on page 170

IF I WERE AN ANIMAL...

The Folks try to live as humans, but their friend
or they would to live us a monkey. If you could
be an animal, what would you be?

I would be:

. . . .

My name would be:

. . . .

I would eat:

. . . .

I would live in:

. . . .

My favourite things to do would be:

. . . .

. . . .

. . . .

HYENA FACTS

The Bolds may live as humans, but they are really hyenas! Here are some amazing facts about hyenas.

In spotted hyena clans, the **girls** are in charge. Female hyenas are **stronger** and more **aggressive** than males.

Hyenas mark their territory by rubbing their **bottoms** on things.

Hyenas have very strong **teeth** that can even bite through **bones**.

Although they look like **dogs**, hyenas are more closely related to **cats**.

Chimps are often thought of as the cleverest animals, but studies show that hyenas are better at problem solving.

You can hear a spotted hyena's laugh from nearly 5km away.

FIFI'S FAVOURITE SONGS

Fifi loves her singing lessons!
Fill in the gaps to complete her favourite
songs, singers and pop groups.

(How Much Is)
That _____ In
The _____?

_____ Love

Boney __

Who Let The
_____ Out?

_____ Dogg

Ain't Nothin' But A
_____ Dog

Dog_____
Are Over

33

answers on page 170

CROSSWORD

Across

1) The Bolds _____ Betty from Dog-Mad Debby.

5) Mrs Bold makes lots of these for her stall.

6) Bobby and Betty ____their tails at school.

7) Mr McNumpty is a particular kind of bear.

9) A piece in Uncle Tony's favourite game.

10) The Bolds' friend Pam is this kind of bird.

Down

2) The snappiest ever resident of the Bolds' house.

3) The illustrator of the Bold books.

4) The Bolds live at number 41 _____ Road.

8) The Bolds' French friend.

Uncle Tony loves crossword puzzles! Solve the Bold clues to complete this one.

TEST YOUR KNOWLEDGE

How well do you remember The Bolds?

Try some tricky trivia to find out!

1) What were Mr and Mrs Bold's names when they lived as hyenas?

    a) Sue and Spot

    b) Haha and Hehe

    c) Fred and Amelia

2) What car do the Bolds have?

    a) Blue Honda Jazz

    b) Red Vauxhall Corsa

    c) Silver Ford Escort

3) What is Mr McNumpty's first name?

    a) Kevin

    b) Brian

    c) Nigel

4) When did Bobby and Betty find out that they were hyenas?

    a) When they were starting school

    b) On their 8th birthday

    c) They've always known

5) Who is the first human to learn the Bolds' secret?

    a) Mrs Dobson

    b) Minnie

    c) Peter, their postman

6) Which safari park is Uncle Tony rescued from?

    a) Kenton

    b) Coulsdon

    c) Morton

7) What is Minnie's dad's job?

    a) Butcher

    b) Baker

    c) Candlestick maker

8) Who sneaks out of the park with Uncle Tony?

    a) Boo

    b) Miranda

    c) Sheila

answers on page 171

CHRISTMAS WISHES

The Bolds have been writing their present wish lists
for Father Christmas. What's on yours? Put your
wishes here in words and pictures.

HOW TO BE HUMAN

When the Bolds find lots of animal visitors,
they held lessons to teach them how
to disguise themselves as humans.

THERE ARE SOME EXAMPLES OF THEIR LESSONS.

TABLE MANNERS
How to master
knives, forks
and spoons.

NAPKINS
These are for wiping
your mouth, please
note, and not to put on
your head or to wipe
your bottoms with!

**WALKING ON
HIND LEGS**
All about balance.
Tricky to begin with,
but essential if you are
to appear in public.

TOILET TRAINING
How to use the toilet
facility, sit on the
toilet seat, use toilet
paper and 'flush'
when you've finished.

DRESSING UP
How to put together
an outfit that looks
human, and can hide
tails, ears, hairy
backs, scaly skin
and so on.

40

What other lessons do you think these
animals would need to learn? Write
some plans for lessons of your own.

HYENA FICTION

Unfortunately, there are lots of myths and legends about hyenas, causing people to think that they are unlucky or evil.

In the Middle Ages, people believed that hyenas dug up and ate dead bodies.

There is an Ethiopian tale of people who have an evil eye and turn themselves into hyenas.

Medieval Europeans believed in the leucrotta – a half-hyena half-lion creature which would lure travellers into danger.

Tanzanian and Indian legends say that witches ride hyenas.

People often think of hyenas as cowardly scavengers, but they are actually excellent hunters, and lions often steal their prey.

INTERVIEW WITH THE CREATORS

Find out what the author and illustrator, Julian Clary and David Roberts, really think of the Bolds.

Who is your favourite character?

JC: My favourite character in the whole of the *Bolds* series is quite an incidental character, Miss Paulina, who is an otter who would like to be a nun. She wears a wimple made out of a tea towel.

DR: I particularly like the character of Mr McNumpty who lives next door to the Bolds. In the first book they're quite suspicious of him, but he's got a secret as well.

What's your favourite illustration?

DR: My favourite illustration in the books would probably be of a character called Roger the sheep. He gets very confused

between his lessons for table manners and toilet training. So I'll let you guess what happens when he sits down for dinner!

Who's your favourite villain?

JC: My favourite villain is in *The Bolds on Holiday*. Dog-Mad Debby, this awful woman who goes around stealing dogs. She's not the cleanest or the most attractive woman, but she was great fun to write. I quite like writing the words that come out of evil people's mouths.

DR: Villains are great to draw as well. One of my favourites is probably in *The Bolds in Trouble*, Mossy the fox. It was wonderful to be able to draw foxes, and especially a villainous fox because you can get a really sly look on its face.

THE BOLDS AWARDS

My favourite Bolds book is...

· ·

My favourite Bolds character is...

· ·

The funniest moment in the Bolds is...

· ·

If I could be a Bold I would be...

· ·

The scariest moment in the Bolds is...

. . . .

The animal character I miss the most is...

. . . .

The bravest character in the Bolds is...

. . . .

The animal in the Bolds books with the best
disguise is...

. . . .

KNOCK KNOCK

Mr Bold loves to put Knock Knock jokes in his crackers, here are some favourites!

Knock, knock!

Who's there?

Mary

Mary who?

Mary Christmas.

CHRISTMAS AROUND THE WORLD

The Belch have friends and family all over the world! Can you match these Christmas traditions to the correct countries?

☐ (A) Iceland

☐ (B) Japan

☐ (C) Philippines

☐ (D) Sweden

☐ (E) Ukraine

☐ (F) Germany

☐ (G) Norway

☐ (H) Venezuela

☐ (I) Spain

1. Families all sit down to watch Donald Duck cartoons on Christmas Eve.

2. Lots of people eat KFC for Christmas dinner.

3. Children are not allowed to see the Christmas tree until 24th December.

4. Trees are decorated with spider web ornaments for good luck.

5. Children are brought their presents by the Three Wise Men, not Santa Claus.

6. People hide their brooms on Christmas Eve to stop witches and evil spirits from riding them.

7. Christmas is celebrated with a beautiful lantern festival.

8. People travel to church on Christmas Eve by rollerblading.

9. People exchange gifts of books on Christmas Eve, and spend the rest of the night reading.

51

answers on page 171

HAT DESIGN

Remember, Mrs Bold uses material such as egg boxes, clothes pegs and birds' nests.

MAZE

Can you draw a trail to help
Uncle Tony escape the safari park?

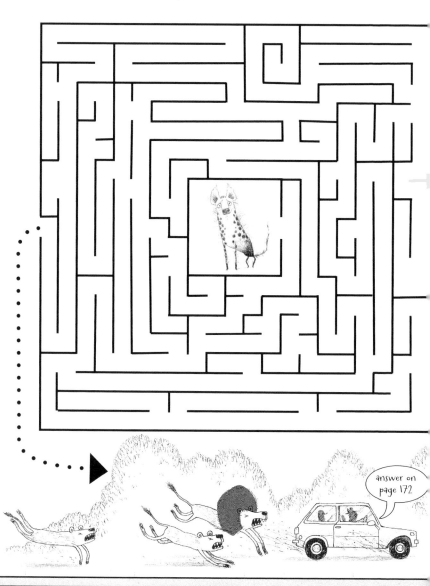

answer on page 172

ODD ONE OUT

Who doesn't fit in this group and why?

Fifi

Roger

Mr McNumpty

Sheila

Gangster's Moll

answer ·

answer on page 172

CAREERS ADVICE

As part of their lessons for animals who wish to be humans, the Folds offer Careers Advice to help their friends figure out what they might like to do in the human world.

(A) Gardener

(F) Nun

(B) Mechanic

(G) Traffic warden

(C) Joke writer

(H) Brewer

(D) Nanny

(I) Singer

(E) Hat maker

Can you match the animal's skills to the job that would most suit them?

1. Amelia is very creative and has good people (and animal) skills.

2. Fred never stops laughing.

3. Roger is very nurturing, and doesn't mind cleaning up other people's messes.

4. Gangster's Moll and Minty Boy love fresh air and nibbling grass.

5. Fifi Lampadaire the poodle is very confident and loves to be the centre of attention.

6. Paulina the otter is very thoughtful and caring.

7. Snappy the goose is fierce and good at telling people off.

8. Craig the wild boar likes to experiment in the kitchen with truffles.

9. Bert the fox is good at fixing things.

answers on page 172

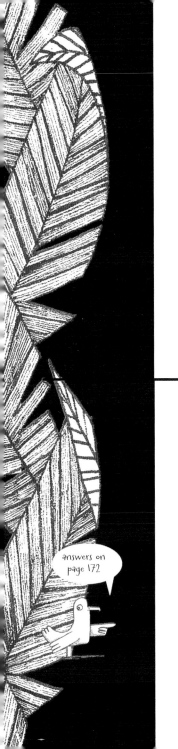

answers on page 172

SPOT THE DIFFERENCE

In all the fun and disguise of the fete, the animals have changed a bit!

Can you find 10 differences between the pictures?

CRYPTIC CODES

Someone's just revealed a shocking secret!
Crack the code to find out what it is.

A	B	C	D	E	F	G	H	I
15	4	24	16	11	18	6	23	26

J	K	L	M	N	O	P	Q	R
12	1	3	22	17	14	21	8	7

S	T	U	V	W	X	Y	Z	
19	5	2	10	25	9	13	20	

__ __ __ __ __ __ __   __ __ __ __ __   __ __
12 11 18 18 7 11 13   25 15 17 5 19   5 14

__ __   __   __ __ __ __ __ __ __ __ __ __
4 11   15   24 23 26 22 21 15 17 20 11 11

answer on page 173

FAMILY LOGO

The Bolds' logo is on all of their books. Can you design a logo for your own family? You could use your surname, or some pictures to symbolise your relatives.

WORDSEARCH

The Dahls were ruined financially at the same reindeer friends this Christmas, but there's nine get your revenge, but here comes one!

R	D	U	Y	T	X	R	L	I	N	S	R
J	I	G	Q	B	E	A	J	E	B	D	E
Q	P	W	L	O	H	M	Z	S	W	A	C
S	U	V	I	K	Z	T	O	K	T	N	N
D	C	B	I	S	I	Z	B	C	V	C	A
B	A	R	E	L	W	W	P	D	M	E	R
G	I	S	B	S	X	U	O	M	B	R	P
N	C	F	H	M	X	N	M	Y	V	K	J
B	J	K	S	E	N	E	X	I	V	F	K
A	W	C	E	E	R	R	J	K	Y	O	N
Z	M	M	R	Q	I	P	Y	Z	G	D	N
R	U	D	O	L	P	H	S	W	C	J	D

Can you find all nine
of their names?

answers on
page 173

TEST YOUR KNOWLEDGE

How well do you remember
The Bolds to the Rescue?

Try some
tricky trivia
to find out!

1) What kind of animal are Gangster's
Moll and Minty Boy?
- a) Horses
- b) Hedgehogs
- c) Hares

2) Which river does Fifi's boat travel along?
- a) Amazon
- b) Mississippi
- c) Nile

3) What's the name of the Bolds' sheep guest?
- a) Shaun
- b) Peter
- c) Roger

answers on page 173

4) Where do the animals go for a day out?

    a) The farm

    b) Bowling

    c) A fete

5) How does Sheila arrive at Fairfield Road?

    a) Flies through the window

    b) Climbs down the chimney

    c) Swims up through the toilet

6) Who captures two of the animals?

    a) Troublesome Trev

    b) Dodgy Dean

    c) Scary Stu

7) Which police officers give the Bolds a fright?

    a) PC Pete and PC Bernard

    b) PC Tim and PC Tina

    c) PC Susan and PC Barbara

8) Which animals save the day with their poo?

    a) Seagulls

    b) Hyenas

    c) Mice

YOU'VE BEEN FRAMED

The Bolds love to hang family photographs and interesting signs on their living room wall. Fill in the rest of the frames with pictures of their friends or sayings of your own.

NEVER TROUBLE
TROUBLE TILL
TROUBLE
TROUBLES YOU!

THE BOLDS

DINGBATS

Mr Told is scratching his head at these dingbats. Help him to find a well-known phrase or saying by saying what you see.

For example:
VA DERS

would be **Space Invaders**
(space in vaders).

GSEG

....

BEND
DRAW
DRAW
DRAW

....

WISH
*

....

5
^

^

^

....

THE
WEATHER
FEELING

....

 answers on page 174

GREAT GIFTS

answers on page 174

Can you match the characters with the Christmas presents they received in *The Bolds*?

(A) Tony

(B) Miranda

(C) Bobby and Betty

(D) Mr and Mrs Bold

(1) Book about Africa

(2) Skipping rope

(3) Mittens

(4) Roller skates

Draw a picture of each gift.

WORD SUDOKU

Bobby and Betty are trying out making a bigger puzzle, using Minnie's pet for inspiration!

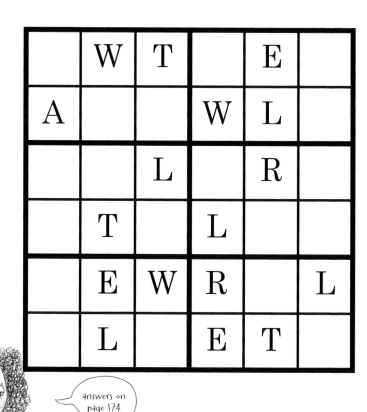

	W	T		E	
A			W	L	
		L		R	
	T		L		
	E	W	R		L
	L		E	T	

answers on page 174

70

Can you fill in the grid so that every row, column and 3x2 square contains each letter from WALTER?

WORD PLAY

Place as many words as you can make from the letters of this festive greeting!

MERRY CHRISTMAS

. . . .

. . . .

. . . .

. . . .

. . . .

Bonus points
for words related
to the Bolds or
Christmas!

RIDDLE ME THIS

What gets wetter and wetter the more it dries?

. . . .

What starts with 't', ends with 't' and has 't' in it?

. . . .

What comes once in a minute, twice in a moment, but never in a thousand years?

. . . .

What's full of holes but can still hold water?

. . . .

What kind of tree can you carry in your hand?

. . . .

A man switches off all the lights in his home and goes to sleep. By the time he wakes up, he has killed six people. How?

. . . .

BETTY'S ANIMAL JOKES

What did one pig say to
the other?
'Let's be pen pals.'

What happened to the chick
that misbehaved at school?
It was eggspelled.

What do you get if you cross
a chicken with a cow?
Roost beef.

Where do horses live?
In the neigh-bourhood.

What time is it when an
elephant sits on your fence?
Time to get a new fence.

What do you call a bear
with no teeth?
A gummy bear.

What do you call a deer
with no eyes?
No idea.

How does a hedgehog
play leap-frog?
Very carefully.

What do you
get if you cross a
kangaroo with
a sheep?

A woolly
jumper.

Why do bees have sticky hair?

Because they use honeycombs.

What kind of bears like to go out in the rain?
Drizzly bears.

What is a cheetah's favourite food?
Fast food.

What did the banana do when the monkey chased it?
The banana split.

What do you get when you pour hot water down a rabbit hole?
Hot cross bunnies.

What did the spider do on the computer?
It made a website.

Why don't dogs make good dancers?
Because they have two left feet.

What dog loves to take bubble baths?
A shampoodle.

What happened to the hyena who swallowed an OXO cube?
He made a laughing stock of himself.

AT THE VET'S

How many animals can you spot in the waiting room?

answer on page 174

HIDING IN PLAIN SIGHT

Sometimes animals in the bible books love
to hide themselves by acting as objects.

Sheila the crocodile was
a stylish handbag.

Minty Bay and
Gangster's Moll
made a glamorous
pair of lamps.

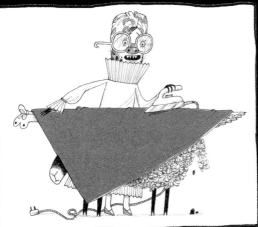

Reggie the sheep
was double-job as an
ironing board.

Think of household object disguises for other animals, and draw them here.

WORDSEARCH

Reading and writing lessons aren't going too well
for the Bolds' newest recruit, Kirsty the cow.
Can you show her where these words are hiding?

L	Y	W	Y	D	A	A	C	P	S	Q	Q
A	P	O	K	W	I	M	N	T	T	T	Y
U	B	U	P	O	J	S	A	E	R	L	R
G	Z	M	P	F	J	H	G	O	Y	Z	F
H	E	U	C	S	E	R	U	U	A	H	D
I	N	N	Q	V	X	B	H	A	I	B	I
N	P	I	O	V	L	J	N	T	F	S	Y
G	B	P	K	E	F	U	Y	D	Y	S	E
T	E	D	D	I	N	G	T	O	N	L	D
S	R	C	Q	P	Y	T	Q	A	U	I	C
D	E	R	R	C	N	J	W	W	G	A	D
T	W	I	L	D	X	L	A	Z	Q	T	Y

HYENA   TAILS
TEDDINGTON   RESCUE
HATS   WILD
DISGUISE   PUPS
LAUGHING   TROUBLE

80   answers on
     page 175

LOST LABELS

Mr Bold is writing labels for family Christmas presents. Can you unscramble the letters for him?

DRIAAMN

. . . .

MIEINN

. . . .

NOYT

. . . .

IELAAM

. . . .

GLNEI

. . . .

UMIMA

. . . .

answers on page 175

CARD CREATION

Design a Christmas card for the Bolds to send out to their friends and family around the world.

The twins have learned a new game at school this term. Change one letter each time to make a new word, eventually arriving at the word on the bottom rung.

For example:

TEN
TON
TOY
JOY

Now try:

GIFT
LOVE

FESTIVE FAVOURITES

The Bolds are always disagreeing over what the best parts of Christmas are. Think about your answers and debate them with your family and friends!

My favourite Christmas song is...

· ·

My favourite Christmas film is...

· ·

My favourite Christmas book is...

· ·

My favourite Christmas advert is...

· ·

The best Christmas present I've ever received is...

. . . .

My favourite festive tradition is...

. . . .

My favourite food at Christmas is...

. . . .

My favourite thing to do in the school holidays is...

. . . .

My favourite Christmas decoration is...

. . . .

My favourite Christmas event is...

. . . .

MAZE

Sylvie has lost her cubs in the park! Draw her a path to follow so the family can be reunited.

START

answer on page 176

ELF IN DISGUISE

An elf is trying to blend in with safari animals
while delivering presents. Can you draw her
in an animal disguise?

TEST YOUR KNOWLEDGE

How well do you remember The Bolds on Holiday?
Try some tricky trivia to find out!

1) Where did the Bolds go on holiday?
   - a) Corfu
   - b) Colombia
   - c) Cornwall

2) What is Minnie's dog called?
   - a) Walter
   - b) Winston
   - c) Wanda

3) What Sports Day event do the twins compete in?
   - a) Hula hooping
   - b) Three-legged race
   - c) Hurdles

answers on page 176

4) What is Bobby's undercover name?
  - a) Trumpy
  - b) Fleabag
  - c) Rover

5) What did Mr Bold forget to pack?
  - a) Tents
  - b) Pyjamas
  - c) Sleeping bags

6) What is the name of Bertha's business?
  - a) Shop by the Sea
  - b) Tiddles Tea Shop
  - c) Crabby Café

7) Who kidnaps animals?
  - a) Lemur-Loving Lucy
  - b) Dog-Mad Debby
  - c) Cat-Crazy Carol

8) What's the name of the helpful dolphin?
  - a) Galileo
  - b) Da Vinci
  - c) Newton

DREAM DESTINATIONS

The Babes went on a fun and trouble-filled holiday to Cornwall. Think about your dream holiday.

I would go to:

. . . .

I would travel by:

. . . .

I would go with:

. . . .

I would stay in:

. . . .

Things I would do:

. . . .

. . . .

or friends enjoying
the holiday.

CROSSWORD

Mr McNumpty needs a break from Fairfield Road Christmas chaos, so it's time for a cup of tea and a festive crossword!

Down

1) Kiss under the _____.
2) Don't forget to open your chocolate calendar.
3) Santa uses this to enter your house.
4) Season's _____.
5) A traditional Christmas roast.
7) A caroller's favourite activity.

Across

4) At Christmas, people exchange these.
6) The _____ and the ivy.
7) Sits at the top of the Christmas tree.
8) A place to keep presents.

93

answers on page 176

ODD ONE OUT

Who doesn't fit in this group and why?

Imamu

Bobby

answer on page 177

Fred

Amelia

Betty

answer ....

94

WORD SUDOKU

Sheila the crocodile got a bit snappy with the twins, wanting a puzzle of her own.

E					I
	H	A	L	S	
H	A	I	E	L	S
S					H
	I	S	H	E	
A					L

Can you fill in the grid so that every row, column and 3x2 square contains each letter from

SHEILA?

answers on page 177

BOLD STROKES

Use the grid to copy this picture of Minnie.

Study each box carefully as you go.

COLOURING CHAOS

Use lots of colour to brighten up
the Bolds' trip to the playground.

AMELIA BOLD

. . . .

. . . .

. . . .

. . . .

. . . .

Bonus points for words related to the Bolds or Christmas!

100

GET A REINDEER READY

Rudolph wants to visit the Bolds!

Can you draw a picture of the reindeer in a human disguise, so he can fit in in Teddington?

answers on page 178

COOKING UP A STORM

On holiday in Cornwall, Mrs Bold made
a meal called Chef's Surprise, which she
made with *everything* she could find.

Ingredients:

Two tins of baked beans

Six eggs

A bar of chocolate

Half a loaf of sliced bread

A litre of semi-skimmed milk

A dozen cooked sausages

Some strawberries

A bag of Brussels sprouts (uncooked)

A packet of biscuits

Three big packets of prawn cocktail crisps

A bottle of tomato ketchup

A jar of peanut butter

Half a bottle of lemonade

Recipe:

1) Put all the ingredients in a large bowl.

2) Mix it all well.

3) Simmer in a saucepan on a low heat for
twenty minutes.

4) Add salt and pepper to taste.

5) Serve in a bowl on the floor, animal-style.

What would you put in your own special Chef's Surprise?

Ingredients:

Recipe:

RIDDLE ME THIS

What fruit is a cross between an apple and a Christmas tree?

. . . .

Which one of Santa's reindeer also works on Valentine's Day?

. . . .

If it takes five elves five minutes to make five dolls, how long would it take 100 elves to make 100 dolls?

. . . .

Where does Christmas come before Halloween?

. . . .

answers on page 179

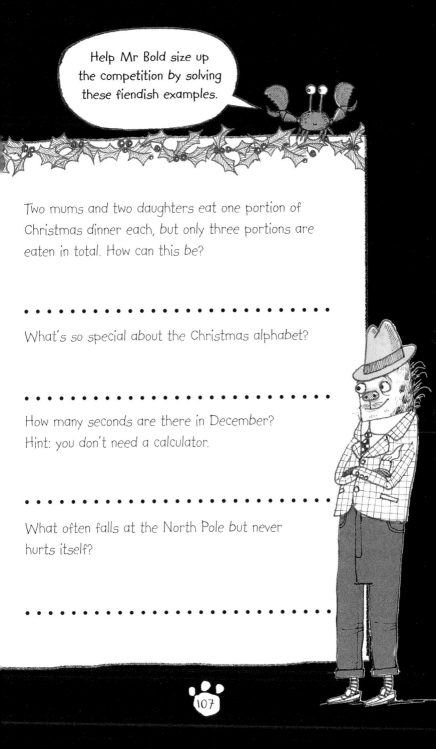

Help Mr Bold size up the competition by solving these fiendish examples.

Two mums and two daughters eat one portion of Christmas dinner each, but only three portions are eaten in total. How can this be?

. . . .

What's so special about the Christmas alphabet?

. . . .

How many seconds are there in December?
Hint: you don't need a calculator.

. . . .

What often falls at the North Pole but never hurts itself?

. . . .

WORD LADDER

The Bolds have been using this game to
practise their human spelling!

GOLD
BELL

Change one letter each
time to make a new word,
eventually arriving at the
word on the bottom rung.

108

answers on
page 179

SAFARI SCRAMBLE

These animals have got their letters
all mixed up, can you unscramble them to
work out what they are?

PANTHEEL

INOL

BRAZE

TREGI

RAGFIFE

INGENUP

POTRRA

ABOBON

answers on page 179

Mr Bold likes to mix up his creative cracker fillings, and sometimes puts in limericks instead of jokes. Here are some of his best examples:

There once was a man from Peru
Who dreamt that he swallowed his shoe.
He woke up in fright
In the midst of the night
To learn that his dream had come true!

A mouse in her room woke Miss Dowd
She was frightened – it must be allowed.
Soon a happy thought hit her –
To scare off the critter,
She sat up in bed and meowed!

There was an old man with a beard
Who said "It's just as I feared!
Two owls and a hen
Four larks and a wren
Are making a nest in my beard!"

There once was a hyena called Tony...

....

....

....

....

There lived a marmoset monkey...

....

....

....

....

There was a family of Bolds...

....

....

....

....

UNCLE CHRISTMAS

Uncle Tony is going to be Santa Claus in a local play. Draw him in his costume.

WORDSEARCH

Imamu is unimpressed by the twins' civilised human writing, and has mixed it all up in protest! Can you find all the words relating to the Bolds?

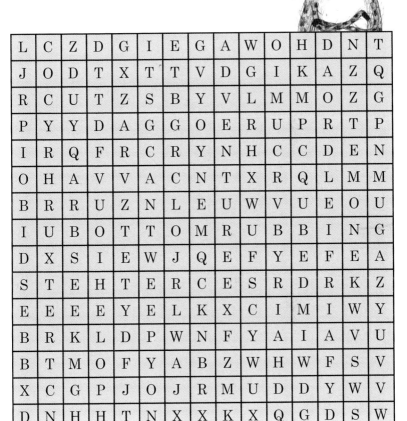

L	C	Z	D	G	I	E	G	A	W	O	H	D	N	T
J	O	D	T	X	T	T	V	D	G	I	K	A	Z	Q
R	C	U	T	Z	S	B	Y	V	L	M	M	O	Z	G
P	Y	Y	D	A	G	G	O	E	R	U	P	R	T	P
I	R	Q	F	R	C	R	Y	N	H	C	C	D	E	N
O	H	A	V	V	A	C	N	T	X	R	Q	L	M	M
B	R	R	U	Z	N	L	E	U	W	V	U	E	O	U
I	U	B	O	T	T	O	M	R	U	B	B	I	N	G
D	X	S	I	E	W	J	Q	E	F	Y	E	F	E	A
S	T	E	H	T	E	R	C	E	S	R	D	R	K	Z
E	E	E	E	Y	E	L	K	X	C	I	M	I	W	Y
B	R	K	L	D	P	W	N	F	Y	A	I	A	V	U
B	T	M	O	F	Y	A	B	Z	W	H	W	F	S	V
X	C	G	P	J	O	J	R	M	U	D	D	Y	W	V
D	N	H	H	T	N	X	X	K	X	Q	G	D	S	W

BUSHY PARK   HAIRY   LOUD
ADVENTURE   HUMAN   FAIRFIELD ROAD
JOKES   SECRET   BOTTOM RUBBING
SAFARI   MUDDY

113

answers on page 180

CHRISTMAS FOR
BEGINNERS

Some of the folks' animal friends and family are coming
to visit for the festive season. They're coming from the
Serengeti, and they've never seen a human Christmas.

WALK OF FAME

answer on page 180

It looks like Fifi needs some help achieving her goals.
Figure out which path she should follow to stardom.

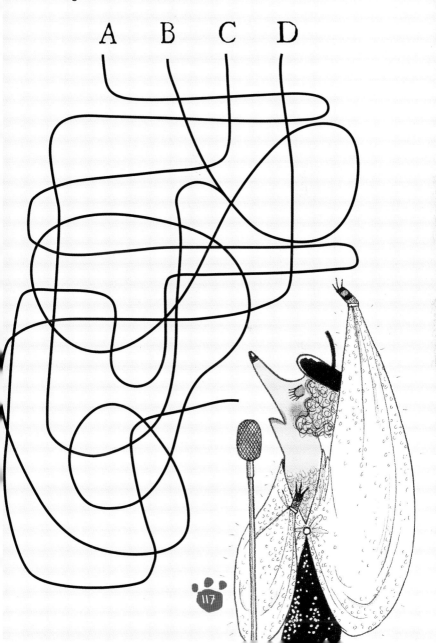

AMAZING ANIMAL FACTS

Impress your friends with surprising facts
about the Bolds' animal friends!

Animals such as **dogs**, cats, horses and cows can suffer from sunburn.

Giraffes have four stomachs.

There are more than 400 million **dogs** in the world.

Killer whales are actually **dolphins**.

Grizzly bears can be up to 8ft tall when they stand on their hind legs.

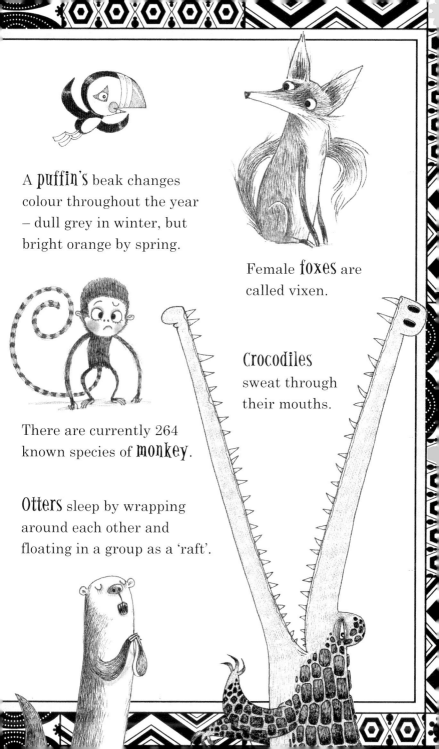

A **puffin's** beak changes colour throughout the year – dull grey in winter, but bright orange by spring.

Female **foxes** are called vixen.

Crocodiles sweat through their mouths.

There are currently 264 known species of **monkey**.

Otters sleep by wrapping around each other and floating in a group as a 'raft'.

COMIC CAPERS

Uncle Tony wakes up to discover that Miranda is missing! What will happen next?

TEST YOUR KNOWLEDGE

How well do you remember The Bolds in Trouble?
Try some tricky trivia to find out!

1) What does Miss Paulina want to be?
   a) Mechanic
   b) Princess
   c) Nun

2) Who are the Bolds' busybody neighbours?
   a) The Browns
   b) The Binghams
   c) The Buxtons

3) What do the twins use for a prank on Uncle Tony?
   a) Pickle
   b) Mustard
   c) Ketchup

4) What's the name of the female fox?
   a) Sylvie
   b) Myrtle
   c) Sheila

answers on page 180

5) What does Craig use to cover his boar ears?
   a) Beanie
   b) Headscarf
   c) Bowler hat

6) What are foxes scared of?
   a) Cougar poo
   b) Lion poo
   c) Hyena poo

7) Who fixes the Bolds' car?
   a) Snappy
   b) Mossy
   c) Bert

8) What are Mrs Bold's most successful hats made of?
   a) Mud
   b) Fish nets
   c) Books

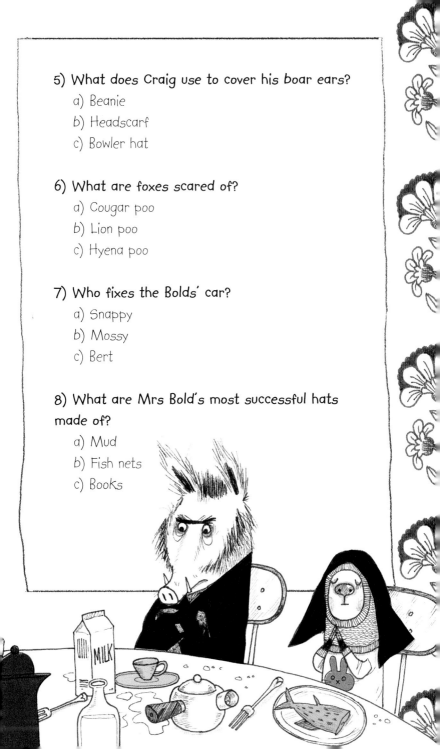

answer on page 180

HOME COMFORTS

The Bolds love their home at 41 Fairfield Road.

> Draw a picture of your dream home and write a description of it.

My dream home is called... . . . .

It is located... . . . .

It is made of... . . . .

The best room is... . . . .

My bedroom would be decorated with...

. . . .

. . . .

Outside, it would have...

. . . .

. . . .

The best object in my home would be...

. . . .

. . . .

WORD SUDOKU

The Bolds think Hector might be their cleverest
friend, so they thought he'd suit a difficult puzzle!

E		O			C
	R	C			
C			O	H	T
		H	R	C	E
R	C	E			
	H				R

Can you fill in the grid so
that every row, column
and 3x2 square contains
each letter from

HECTOR?

answers on
page 181

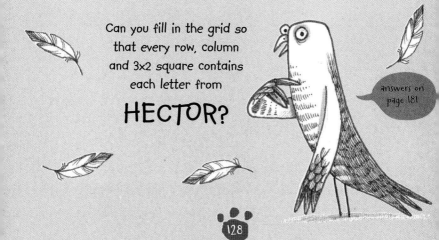

128

DINGBATS

YYY MEN	Mistletoe XXX
....	....
PPPPP Planet	sTel
....	....
Hi Spring! Hey Summer! Hello Autumn! Goodbye Winter!	S N O W
....	....

answers on page 181

HUMAN ERROR

When the Rolds and their friends first started their lives as humans, they made lots of silly mistakes!

- 🐾 They learned the hard way that shampoo was *not* a refreshing fruity drink.

- 🐾 They thought the hoover was a musical instrument.

- 🐾 They kept their underwear in the fridge.

- 🐾 They ate toothpaste for breakfast.

- 🐾 They used butter as moisturiser.

- 🐾 They tried to eat dinner with an umbrella.

- 🐾 And there have been more than a couple of toilet incidents...

animal might guess these objects are used for? Draw some illustrations to show them.

CROSSWORD

Billy and Patty have been given one holiday puzzle to keep them quiet. Solve the clues to help complete the festive crossword!

Down

1) He didn't get to join in any reindeer games.

2) They fall for a white Christmas.

4) Santa's transport.

5) We Three _____.

7) A shiny decoration.

Across

3) Now bring us some figgy
_____.

6) Another word for a Christmas tree.

8) Eight maids-a-_____.

9) Santa's elves make them in their workshop.

10) The _____ days of Christmas .

answers on page 181

THE TWELVE DAYS
OF BOLDSMAS

Use these gifts from your true love
to sing a Bolds version of the
Twelve Days of Christmas.

On the twelfth day of Boldsmas
my true love gave to me...

12 Big disasters

11 Creatures rescued

10 Fancy hats

9 Great adventures

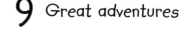

8 Bolds-a-laughing

7 Human disguises

6 Grizzly bears

5 Knock knock jokes

4 Cuckoo birds

3 Monkeys

2 Race horses

And a goose called
Snaaaaaappy

SPOT THE DIFFERENCE

The twins like to play tricks on poor
Mr McNumpty and Uncle Tony!

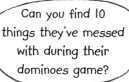

Can you find 10 things they've messed with during their dominoes game?

answers on page 182

ODD ONE OUT

BAUBLE

TINSEL

CANDY CANES

LIGHTS

STOCKINGS

The Bolds are putting up their decorations, but which item doesn't fit in this group and why?

answer

....

answer on page 182

MAZE

Mrs Bold has got lost on her way
to Teddington market, draw a line
to help her get to work.

START

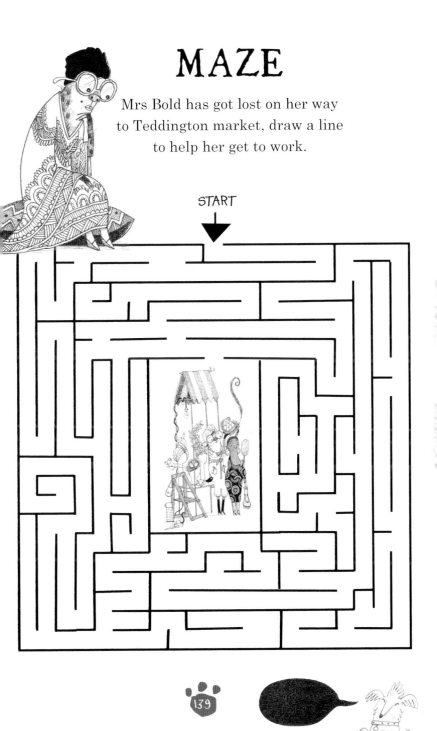

CREATE A COVER

Design your own Bolds cover. Think of a title and a picture for your book.

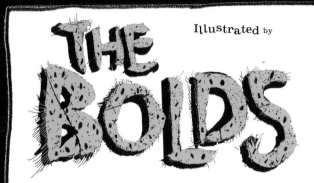

Illustrated by

By

Design a back cover for your Bolds book, and write a blurb to introduce the story.

£

0 705632 441947

www.theboldsbooks.co.uk

MR BOLD'S JOKES

Knock Knock

Who's there?

Tree.

Tree who?

Tree wise men.

ANAGRAMS

Mr Bold's 'innovative' method of decoration storage has caused some problems! Can you unravel the letters to work out what he has put away for next Christmas?

ERET

....

RFYAI LGSITH

....

SBAELUB

....

LITENS

....

WTHERA

....

answers on page 183

STOCKINGS

Design some stockings for the inhabitants to hang up
on the fireplace. Think about what they might find
inside. Maybe a letter, or a toy...

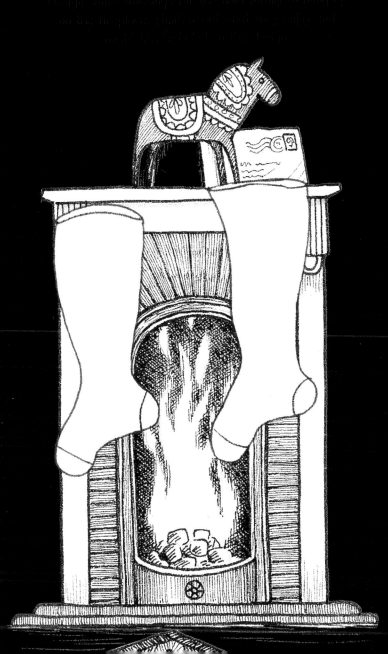

WORD SUDOKU

Mr Bold is utterly stumped by this tricky one!

P	Y	K		B		U	R	
B				Y			S	
U			R				B	
			B	S	Y		A	
R			K					U
		S		A	R	P	H	
S		U			K			H
					B	R		
		R	A	P				

Can you fill in the grid so that every row, column and 3x3 square contains each letter from **BUSHY PARK?**

answers on page 183

WORDSEARCH

Help! Miranda has got the Bolds' friends
all mixed up in a wordsearch! Can you find
the names of 10 characters?

A	C	H	C	G	X	P	C	P	M	Y	S	J	C	Z
H	D	W	D	D	B	E	W	R	K	A	X	F	U	Q
X	A	N	R	N	E	L	M	A	V	B	F	I	M	U
G	S	X	A	I	Z	C	L	I	Y	A	K	F	K	X
B	Y	U	N	R	N	V	E	L	E	P	I	I	C	J
X	W	N	F	U	I	A	T	E	K	O	M	L	Y	L
J	I	R	M	U	Q	M	Z	M	V	L	A	A	C	T
M	E	P	M	Q	B	D	D	A	D	T	M	M	V	B
D	T	Y	N	O	T	E	L	C	N	U	U	P	Q	U
Y	S	Z	N	N	M	U	T	V	N	X	H	A	A	Y
Z	S	I	Q	E	L	F	U	T	H	I	E	D	Q	F
T	Q	D	B	K	M	N	O	A	Y	G	N	A	W	N
D	E	D	E	X	T	Y	K	F	X	P	N	I	B	E
B	O	B	B	Y	R	T	N	U	Z	N	Y	R	K	W
H	A	K	F	B	K	N	N	Q	K	F	L	E	A	D

BOBBY   UNCLE TONY

BETTY   MINNIE

FRED   FIFI LAMPADAIRE

AMELIA   MIRANDA

MR MCNUMPTY   IMAMU

147

answers on
page 184

BOLD STROKES

Use the grid to copy this picture of Pam the puffin.

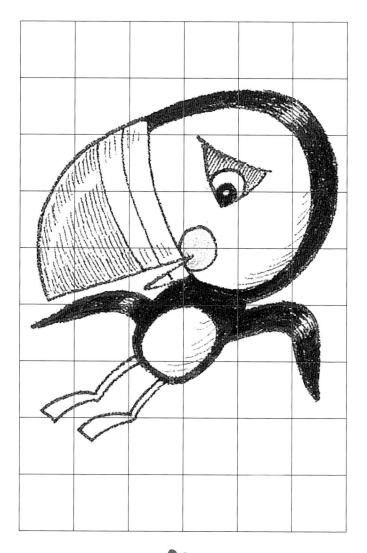

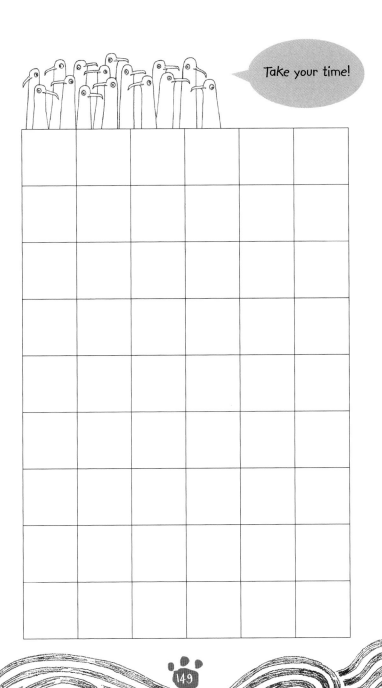

TEST YOUR KNOWLEDGE

How well do you remember
The Bolds Go Wild?
Try some tricky trivia to find out!

answers on
page 184

1) What sort of animal is Hector?
- a) Cuckoo
- b) Puffin
- c) Parrot

2) Where does Imamu live?
- a) Serengeti
- b) Sahara
- c) Seville

3) What is Bobby and Betty's headteacher called?
- a) Mrs Johnson
- b) Mrs Hobson
- c) Mrs Dobson

4) Which celebrity does Imamu meet on her journey
   to Teddington?
   - a) Helena Hardnose
   - b) Kym Kashcow
   - c) Rosa Rolyton

5) Where do the Bolds go to play in the mud?
   - a) Hyde Park
   - b) Bushy Park
   - c) Central Park

6) Which supermodel animal helps Imamu get home?
   - a) Zebra
   - b) Giraffe
   - c) Tiger

7) Which hyena feature finally reveals the twins' secret?
   - a) Ears
   - b) Laugh
   - c) Tails

8) Where do the Bolds go to give Jeffrey
   some monkey practice?
   - a) New Forest
   - b) Forest of Dean
   - c) Lake District

BOLD ACTS

The Bold surname represents how brave and adventurous the family are. Interview your friends and family and ask them about the boldest thing they've ever done. They can be courageous acts, moments of inventiveness or even times when they've been a little bit mischievous.

Name:

Picture:

The Boldest thing I've ever done is...

Name:

Picture:

The Boldest thing I've ever done is...

Name:

Picture:

The Boldest thing I've ever done is...

Imagine this:

A pride of lions is going to attack you. You are running as fast as you can, running for dear life. They are closing in about to pounce. How can you escape from them?

. . . .

I am a horse without legs and a body, I jump but never run. What kind of a horse am I?

. . . .

What kind of mouse would a cat not want to eat?

. . . .

Minnie is writing some riddles inspired by her wild friends. See if you can work them out!

A chicken was given £6, an ant was given £18 and a spider was given £24. How much money was the dog given?

. . . .

I have the exact same size and shape as a hippopotamus but I weigh nothing. What am I?

. . . .

Most of the time I am big, scary and hairy and can strike terror in those that I go after. Yet I have one form in which I am colourful, small and kids love to gobble me up. What animal am I?

. . . .

155

answers on page 184

WORD LADDER

The animal inhabitants of Teddington have to disguise themselves from head to tail, but can you get between the two in this puzzle?

HEAD
TAIL

Change one letter each time to make a new word, eventually arriving at the word on the bottom rung.

answers on page 184

TRUE OR FALSE?

Miranda is getting confused learning about human Christmas. Help her by working out if these statements are true or false!

True False

1) A snowflake has 8 main arms.

2) 'Jingle Bells' was originally called 'One Horse Open Sleigh'.

3) The Statue of Liberty was a Christmas present from France to the USA.

4) It's considered bad luck to take down decorations after New Year's Day.

5) Holly berries are safe to eat.

6) Naughty children get chocolate in their stocking from Santa.

7) A baby reindeer is called a calf.

8) Five types of bird are mentioned in the song 'The Twelve Days of Christmas'.

9) Celebrating Christmas was banned in Britain from 1647 until 1660.

10) There are three towns in the USA named Santa Claus.

157

answers on page 184

CREATURE CREATION

There are lots of animals in the Bolds
that we know about, but can you think
creatively and invent a new animal?

What's it called?

. . . .

Where does it live?

. . . .

What does it eat?

. . . .

How does it move?

. . . .

What skills does it have?

. . . .

Draw a picture of your new creation:

CRYPTIC CODES

Fifi's not the only animal who loves to sing! Can you crack the code and work out each of the Bolds' favourite Christmas songs?

A	B	C	D	E	F	G	H	I	J	K	L	M
9	4	22	15	20	24	5	18	11	16	26	1	2

N	O	P	Q	R	S	T	U	V	W	X	Y	Z
3	21	14	8	13	19	23	6	7	12	25	17	10

MR MCNUMPTY

_ _ _ _ _ _ _ _ _ _ _
19 11 1 20 3 23 3 11 5 18 23

BETTY

_ _ _ _ _ _ _ _ _ _ _
16 11 3 5 1 20 4 20 1 1 19

160

answers on page 185

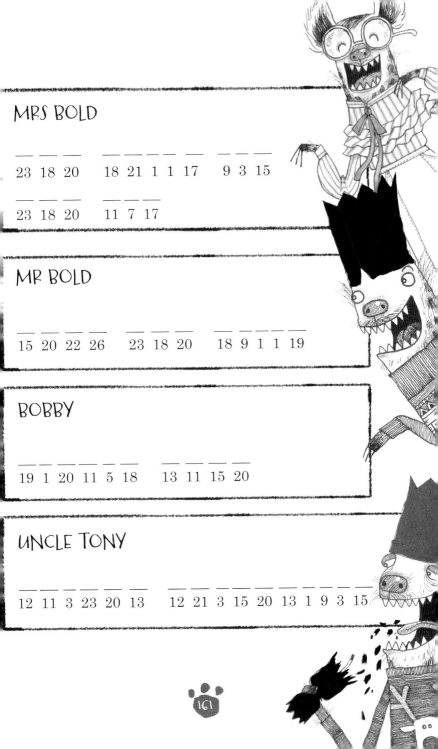

MRS BOLD

__ __ __ __   __ __ __ __ __   __ __ __
23 18 20   18 21 1 1 17   9 3 15

__ __ __ __   __ __ __
23 18 20   11 7 17

MR BOLD

__ __ __ __   __ __ __   __ __ __ __ __
15 20 22 26   23 18 20   18 9 1 1 19

BOBBY

__ __ __ __ __ __   __ __ __ __
19 1 20 11 5 18   13 11 15 20

UNCLE TONY

__ __ __ __ __ __   __ __ __ __ __ __ __ __ __ __
12 11 3 23 20 13   12 21 3 15 20 13 1 9 3 15

Can you spot 10 differences between their versions?

answers on page 185

NEW YEAR'S RESOLUTIONS

At the end of December, lots of people (and animals!) like to make New Year's resolutions, which are personal targets for things they want to achieve in the next twelve months.

Mr Bold is phoning around his friends to find out everyone's ideas.

· **Mr Bold** wants to make more jokes outside of work (everybody else is not so sure).

· **Mrs Bold** wants to branch out her stall into homeware as well as hats.

· **Bobby** is going to try to behave better at school.

· **Betty** wants to improve her football and get onto the school team.

· **Imamu** wants to visit her family in Teddington more often.

· **Uncle Tony** wants to get better at dominoes, so he can stop losing to Mr McNumpty.

· **Miranda** no want eaty vegetables.

Make a list of your own New Year's resolutions.

....

....

....

....

....

....

....

....

....

....

....

....

....

JOKES WANTED

....

....

....

....

....

....

....

....

....

....

....

....

Mr Bold is having joke-writer's block, can you help him come up with some ideas?

167

ANSWERS

P.8/9 SPOT THE DIFFERENCE

P.10 BOLDS TRUE OR FALSE

1) TRUE 2) FALSE 3) FALSE 4) TRUE
5) FALSE 6) TRUE 7) TRUE 8) FALSE
9) FALSE 10) FALSE

P.12 WORDSEARCH

```
S T R D F Z K B I P I R I Y P
N L B M M M I V R A J B K U T
R D L M I N C E P I E S A L I
Y E P E Y S S K O A O C J E N
A G K E B E T G N I K C O T S
D B M C N E L F R I I S I E
I L A T A I L A E E U E U D L
L P S U D R M G K T N H A E T
O R V D B I C A N T O H L Q R
H L U R L L E A I N E C J Q
M P G Y I F E Y O J J Q A I I
E H K F W E K U O J K E T Q P
N I O O S P A B W J L U N F I
P Z N Y L L O H U J O I A L M
Z S C A R O L S S I Y P S I S
```

P.13 SUDOKU

B	O	L	D
L	D	B	O
D	L	O	B
O	B	D	L

169

P.18/19 MUDDLED MEALS

RYKETU Turkey

GINFFSUT Stuffing

IKSERRHOY UGDINDP Yorkshire Pudding

SGPI NI EBLANSTK Pigs in Blankets

PORSTUS Sprouts

OPOTASET Potatoes

ELYU OLG Yule Log

P.21 GLOBAL GREETINGS

A) 3 B) 8 C) 7 D) 6 E) 1 F) 4 G) 2 H) 10
I) 5 J) 9

P.26 CRYPTIC CODES

CHRISTMAS WAS MR BOLD'S FAVOURITE TIME
OF YEAR

P.33 FIFI'S FAVOURITE SONGS

(How Much Is) That **Doggie** In The **Window**?

Puppy Love

Boney **M**

Who Let The **Dogs** Out?

Snoop Dogg

Ain't Nothin' But A **Hound** Dog

Dog **Days** Are Over

P.35 CROSSWORD

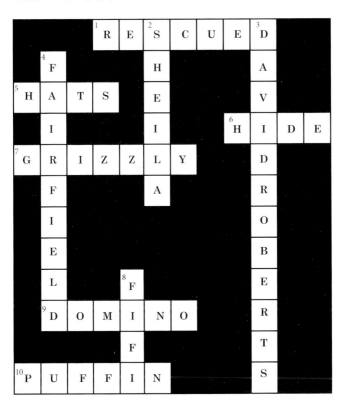

The crossword solution:
- 1 Across: RESCUED
- 2 Down: SHELIA
- 3 Down: DAVDRROBERTS
- 4 Down: FAIFIEL
- 5 Across: HATS
- 6 Across: HIDE
- 7 Across: GRIZZLY
- 8 Down: FF
- 9 Across: DOMINO
- 10 Across: PUFFIN

P.36/7 TEST YOUR KNOWLEDGE

1) A 2) A 3) C 4) A 5) B 6) A 7) A 8) B

P.50/I CHRISTMAS AROUND THE WORLD

1) D 2) B 3) F 4) E 5) I 6) G 7) C 8) H 9) A

P.54 MAZE

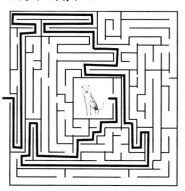

P.55 ODD ONE OUT

Sheila is the only animal who didn't decide to live as a human.

P.56/7 CAREERS ADVICE

A) 4 B) 9 C) 2 D) 3 E) 1 F) 6 G) 7 H) 8 I) 5

P.58/9 SPOT THE DIFFERENCE

P.60 CRYPTIC CODES

JEFFREY WANTS TO BE A CHIMPANZEE

P.63 WORDSEARCH

R	D	U	Y	T	X	R	L	I	N	S	R
J	I	G	Q	B	E	A	J	E	B	D	E
Q	P	W	L	O	H	M	Z	S	W	A	C
S	U	V	I	K	Z	T	O	K	T	N	N
D	C	B	I	S	I	Z	B	C	V	C	A
B	A	R	E	L	W	W	P	D	M	E	R
G	I	S	B	S	X	U	O	M	B	R	P
N	C	F	H	M	X	N	M	Y	V	K	J
B	J	K	S	E	N	E	X	I	V	F	K
A	W	C	E	E	R	R	J	K	Y	O	N
Z	M	M	R	Q	I	P	Y	Z	G	D	N
R	U	D	O	L	P	H	S	W	C	J	D

P.64/5 TEST YOUR KNOWLEDGE

1) A 2) C 3) C 4) C 5) C
6) B 7) A 8) A

173

P.68 DINGBATS

Scrambled eggs · Bend over backwards
Wish upon a star · High five
Feeling under the weather

P.69 GREAT GIFTS

A) 3 B) 2 C) 4 D) 1

P.70 SUDOKU

L	W	T	A	E	R
A	R	E	W	L	T
W	A	L	T	R	E
E	T	R	L	W	A
T	E	W	R	A	L
R	L	A	E	T	W

P.72/3 RIDDLE ME THIS

A towel · A teapot · The letter 'm' · A sponge
A palm· He's a lighthouse keeper

P.76/7 AT THE VET'S

There are 8 animals in the picture.

P.80 WORDSEARCH

```
L Y W Y D A A C P S Q Q
A P O K W I M N T T T Y
U B U P O J S A E R L R
G Z M P F J H G O Y Z F
H E U C S E R U U A H D
I N N Q V X B H A I B I
N P I O V L J N T F S Y
G B P K E F U Y D Y S E
T E D D I N G T O N L D
S R C Q P Y T Q A U I C
D E R R C N J W W G A D
T W I L D X L A Z Q T Y
```

P.81 LOST LABELS

DRIAAMN MIRANDA · MIEINN MINNIE
IELAAM AMELIA · NOYT TONY
GLNEI NIGEL · UMIMA IMAMU

P.83 WORD LADDER

GIFT
LIFT
LIFE
LIVE
LOVE

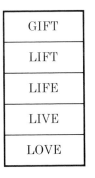

175

P.86 MAZE

P.88/9 TEST YOUR KNOWLEDGE
1) C 2) A 3) B 4) A 5) C 6) B 7) B 8) A

P.93 CROSSWORD

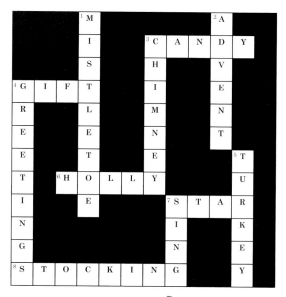

			¹M						²A	
			I		³C	A	N	D	Y	
			S		H				V	
⁴G	I	F	T		I				E	
R			L		M				N	
E			E		N				T	
E			T		E				⁵T	
T		⁶H	O	L	L	Y			U	
I			E			⁷S	T	A	R	
N						I			K	
G						N			E	
⁸S	T	O	C	K	I	N	G		Y	

176

P.94 ODD ONE OUT

Imamu is the only one who doesn't live on Fairfield Road.

P.95 SUDOKU

E	S	L	A	H	I
I	H	A	L	S	E
H	A	I	E	L	S
S	L	E	I	A	H
L	I	S	H	E	A
A	E	H	S	I	L

P.106/7 RIDDLE ME THIS

A pineapple

Cupid

Still five minutes – one elf takes five minutes to make one doll

In the dictionary

It's a grandmother eating with her daughter and granddaughter

There's No-el

Just one – 2nd December

Snow

P.108 WORD LADDER

GOLD
TOLD
TOLL
TELL
BELL

P.109 SAFARI SCRAMBLE

ELEPHANT

LION

ZEBRA

TIGER

GIRAFFE

PENGUIN

PARROT

BABOON

P.113 WORDSEARCH

L	C	Z	D	G	I	E	G	A	W	O	H	D	N	T
J	O	D	T	X	T	T	V	D	G	I	K	A	Z	Q
R	C	U	T	Z	S	B	Y	V	L	M	M	O	Z	G
P	Y	Y	D	A	G	G	O	E	R	U	P	R	T	P
I	R	Q	F	R	C	R	Y	N	H	C	C	D	E	N
O	H	A	V	V	A	C	N	T	X	R	Q	L	M	M
B	R	R	U	Z	N	L	E	U	W	V	U	E	O	U
I	U	B	O	T	T	O	M	R	U	B	B	I	N	G
D	X	S	I	E	W	J	Q	E	F	Y	E	F	E	A
S	T	E	H	T	E	R	C	E	S	R	D	R	K	Z
E	E	E	E	Y	E	L	K	X	C	I	M	I	W	Y
B	R	K	L	D	P	W	N	F	Y	A	I	A	V	U
B	T	M	O	F	Y	A	B	Z	W	H	W	F	S	V
X	C	G	P	J	O	J	R	M	U	D	D	Y	W	V
D	N	H	H	T	N	X	X	K	X	Q	G	D	S	W

P.117 WALK OF FAME

Fifi needs to take path C.

P.122/3 TEST YOUR KNOWLEDGE

1) C 2) B 3) B 4) A 5) C 6) B 7) C 8) A

P.124/5 SUBURBAN SAFARI

There are five disguised animals.

P.128 SUDOKU

E	T	O	H	R	C
H	R	C	E	T	O
C	E	R	O	H	T
T	O	H	R	C	E
R	C	E	T	O	H
O	H	T	C	E	R

P.129 DINGBATS

Three Wise Men • Peace on Earth

Season's Greetings • Kisses Under the Mistletoe

Tinsel ('T' in 'sel') • Snowball

P.132/3 CROSSWORD

P.138 ODD ONE OUT

Stockings are the only ones not used to decorate the Christmas tree.

P.139 MAZE

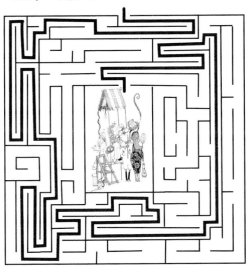

P.144 ANAGRAMS

TREE · FAIRY LIGHTS · BAUBLES
TINSEL · WREATH

P.146 SUDOKU

P	Y	K	S	B	H	U	R	A
B	R	A	P	Y	U	H	S	K
U	S	H	R	K	A	Y	B	P
H	U	P	B	S	Y	K	A	R
R	A	B	K	H	P	S	Y	U
Y	K	S	U	A	R	P	H	B
S	B	U	Y	R	K	A	P	H
A	P	Y	H	U	B	R	K	S
K	H	R	A	P	S	B	U	Y

P.147 WORDSEARCH

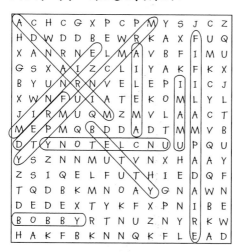

P.150/1 TEST YOUR KNOWLEDGE

1) A 2) A 3) C 4) B 5) B 6) B 7) C 8) A

P.154/5 RIDDLE ME THIS

Stop imagining! · A chess piece · A computer mouse

£12 – £3 per leg · A hippopotamus' shadow

A bear (gummy bears!)

P.156 WORD LADDER

HEAD
HEAL
TEAL
TELL
TALL
TAIL